All Right Already!

A Snowy Story

By Jory John
Illustrated by Benji Davies

HARPER

An Imprint of HarperCollinsPublishers

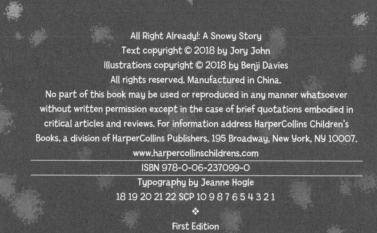

All Right Already!: A Snowy Story
Text copyright © 2018 by Jory John
Illustrations copyright © 2018 by Benji Davies
All rights reserved. Manufactured in China.
No part of this book may be used or reproduced in any manner whatsoever
without written permission except in the case of brief quotations embodied in
critical articles and reviews. For information address HarperCollins Children's
Books, a division of HarperCollins Publishers, 195 Broadway, New York, NY 10007.
www.harpercollinschildrens.com
ISBN 978-0-06-237099-0
Typography by Jeanne Hogle
18 19 20 21 22 SCP 10 9 8 7 6 5 4 3 2 1
❖
First Edition

To Mom, who taught me to appreciate many things,
including bears, ducks, and the snow
—Jory John

For Isaac, Otto, & Rufus
— Benji Davies

"Ah, another magnificent day.
I love my morning routine."

"Wait a minute. Everything looks . . ."

"...*different*.

Goodness gracious, it *snowed*! And not just a little.
It snowed a *lot*."

"I've got to tell Bear! He won't believe it. But it's true, so he'll *have* to believe it."

"Bear! Open up! It's Duck! From next door! It snowed, ol' buddy! Come on outside and have a look."

"Grrr. What is it, Duck?
I'm in the middle of my bath."

"Look around, Bear!
There's snow everywhere.
Let's go exploring."

"Not a chance, Duck.
It's *waaaaaay* too cold
out there."

"Do you want to play freeze tag??"

"No."

"Build a fort?"

"No."

"Make a snowbear?"

"No."

"Come on, Bear. Let's make snow angels together. Then you can go back to sitting around."

"Sigh.

All right already, Duck."

"Okay! Lean back in the snow and move your arms and legs back and forth. Just flap around and . . .

Voilà!"

"Like this?"

"Great. Now let's have a snowball fight."

WHAP!

"Isn't this fun?"

"Not at all."

"Brr. I'm drenched. I'm going home, Duck. Okay? That's quite enough excitement for one day."

"Whatever you need to do, Bear! I'm just glad we got to experience the magic of winter together."

CCCI

COUGH
COUGH
COUGH!

HOOOOOO

RUMBLE
RUMBLE

"Uh-oh."

"Do you want me to wrap you up in blankets?"

"No."

"Make you some soup?"

"No."

"Put a cold compress on your head?"

"No."

"Put a *hot* compress on your head?"

"No."

"Make you some toast?"

"No."

"Tell you a story from my childhood?"

"No."

"Wrap you up in blankets?"

"You already said that."

"Please let me do *something*, Bear."

"ALL R

IGHT ALREADY!

Sigh. How about this: My pillow is flat, Duck.
You can help me with that. Okay?"

"Yes! I'll unflatten your pillow."

"Okay, Duck . . ."

"And make you some tea."

"That's fine . . ."

"And unflatten your pillow."

"You already did that."

"And take your temperature."

"Ugh."

"And read you this magazine."

"No, thanks."

"And feed you some walnuts."

"I'm allergic."

"Duck, you've GOT to let me rest! That's the only way I'm going to get better. Okay? Right now you're not helping me in any way. In fact, you're just making things worse.

Out! Now!"

"All right already, Bear. I'll go home."

"Jeez, Bear's bad attitude is making me feel kind of icky.

COUGH
COUGH,
Sniffle.

Maybe I should make some . . .

AAAAAAH-CHOOOO!

. . . tea, just in case I'm . . . starting to get . . . cough . . . sick myself.

I don't feel so good. I wonder if Bear will notice and come take care of *me*, just like I did for *him*. That would be nice."

PLEASE TAKE CARE OF ME!

"What on Earth is Duck doing?"

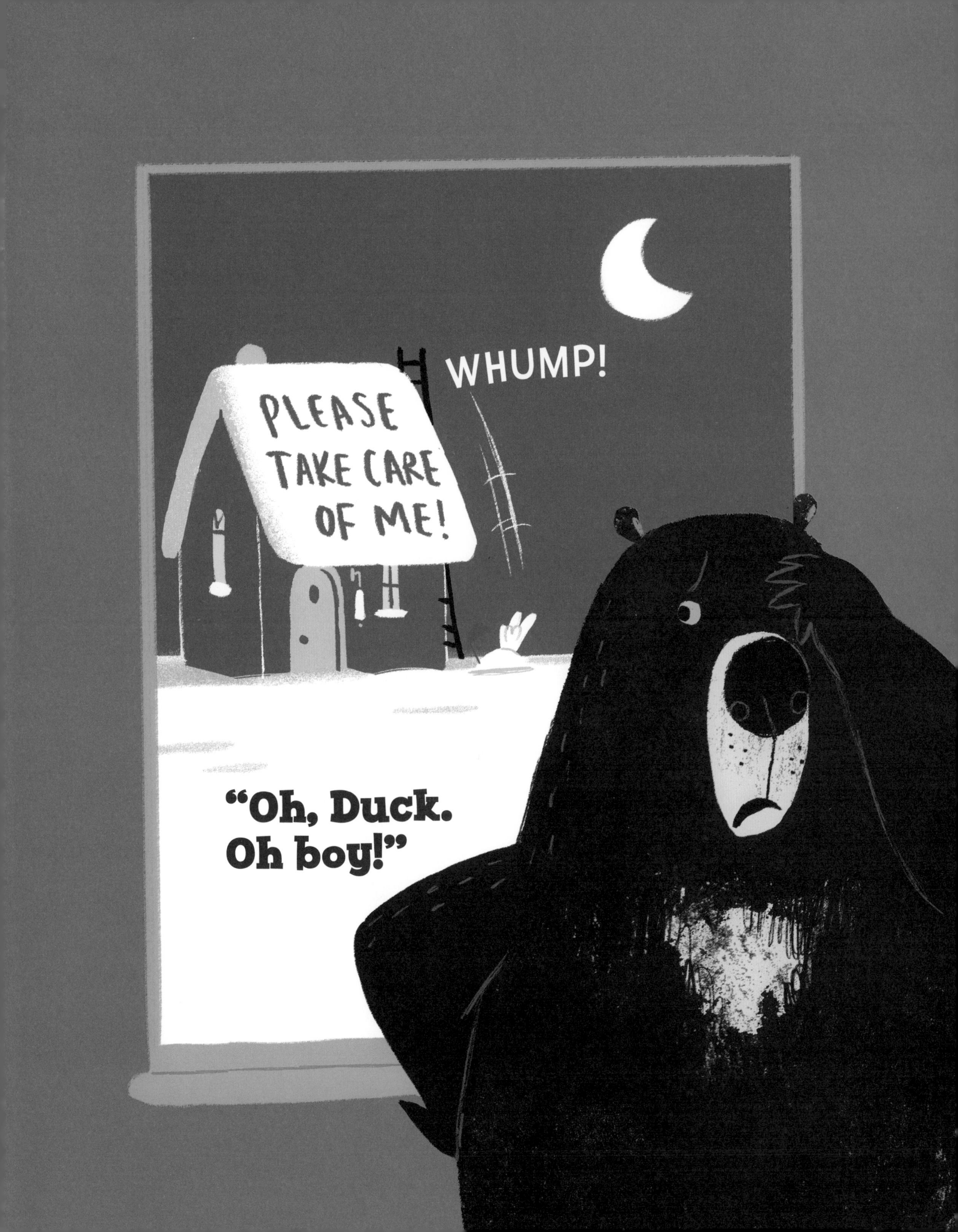

**"Oh, Duck.
Oh boy!"**

"Bear! Oh Bear! You there?"

"Yes, Duck. I'm in your kitchen."

"Oh, good. I like my tea really hot, Bear.

And I'm starting to get a little sore.

And my pillow is flat.
Bear? BEAR!

Are you there, BEAR?!"

"GRRR. ALL RIGHT ALREADY, DUCK.

SNIFF

I *must* get some new neighbors."